THE ADVENTURES OF
WEE ROBERT BRUCE

To my mother, Margaret Hunter (Meg)

Thank you for being such an avid reader and
for passing on your love for books.

THE ADVENTURES OF
WEE ROBERT BRUCE

Best Wishes

Paul H

By Paul V Hunter
Illustrations by Sarah Crome
and Catherine Crome

AUCH ✦ BOOKS

First published in 2012
This edition published in 2014

Text copyright © Paul Hunter
Photographs copyright © Paul Hunter
Illustrations copyright © Sarah Crome

First published in Scotland 2012 by
Auch Books, Bonhill, West Dunbartonshire, Scotland
www.auchbooks.co.uk

British Library catalogue record for this book is
available from the British Library.

ISBN 978-0-9536316-1-2

Book design and artwork by Sarah Crome
Illustrations by Catherine Crome and Sarah Crome
Cover design by Paul Hunter, Peter Montgomery
and Ronnie B. Goodwin
Printed in Scotland by Anderson Printers, Govan, Glasgow

Acknowledgements

I have dedicated this book in memory of my mother Margaret Hunter not only for passing on her love for books, but for the trip to 'Brigadoon' in Burns country when I was a boy. There, I saw for myself where Tam 'O' Shanter was chased on his horse by the witches; a day that opened up my imagination for good and made me look at the world in a different way.

There are many others whom I would like to thank; not least my wonderful dad Victor Hunter, who has steared myself and my family in turbulent times and remains our rock. Many thanks also go to my friend Chris Pollock for his help, support and suggestions and his son Connor Pollock for being our Cover 'Wee Bruce'. Of course, how could I forget Scotland's most famous king, Robert the Bruce? His strength, courage and achievements have been a constant source of inspiration to me.

Finally, a huge debt of gratitude goes to Sarah Crome at Auch Books, for her evocotive illustrations and the wee title pictures from her daughter, Catherine Crome; but also for Sarah's hard work and organisation in making this book a reality and for believing in me.

Paul V Hunter
October 2014

Contents

I.
WEE ROBERT THE BRUCE
by Paul V Hunter

I.

WEE ROBERT THE BRUCE

Wee Robert the Bruce was just like any other wee boy, except for the fact that one day in the future he would be King of all Scotland. His father was also named Robert Bruce, and his father before him. It was a family tradition bestowed on the eldest boy of each generation.

Wee Bruce lived in the parish of Cardross, at the Manor house near to Dumbarton Castle, Dalmoak and Dalreoch. He lived there with his mother Marjorie, his brothers Edward, Nigel, Thomas and Alexander. He also had sisters called Mary, Christina, Margaret and Matilda.

He dreamt of fighting and winning battles, so he carried with him at all times his wooden sword strapped to his side. His uncle the Earl of Lennox made it for him. He needed to be armed all the time to protect Scotland against her enemies from outside, so he trained daily with his trusty weapon.

He was brave and more courageous than all his brothers and no-one ever got the better of him except his dad's favourite hunting hound when it was a pup.

On some occasions he would go hunting with his father and uncles to the wilds of Dalmoak to hunt wild boar with bow and arrow. He enjoyed the hunt, the excitement of the chase, the shouting and screaming and getting dirty in the process. He was brought up on these lands and hunted, fished, hawked and carried wood down to his father's boat anchored in the river Leven near to the Manor house. This was the river where he learned to swim when he was very young, where he caught his first salmon and trout and was chased out of the water by huge pike showing off their razor sharp teeth.

Many a time he nearly drowned, especially during the winter months but always somehow managed to reach the safety of the riverbank. Wrapped up in warm dry furs and drying off by the huge fire, he would be told off by his mother for spending so much time out in the cold. She said that one day it would be the death of him, but he never listened. Life was too exciting and he had way too much energy to sit around the house.

One day he overheard his brothers discussing a plot of land across the water called '*the lions gate.*' This was a place his father warned him never to go because it was dangerous.

He kept a huge lion in a deep pit under the ground that devoured men. He never dared to go before and to enter lions gate he had to pass the home of the holy men called *Culdees*. These were monks with special powers that could control the weather and turn men into beasts. They frightened the young boy, and he kept away from them as much as he could. If spotting them when outside roaming the land he would turn and walk in the other direction.

He used to have bad dreams about them. He never bothered about them until one day when he was passing with his parents, an old wrinkly, mysterious Culdee told him that one day he would be the greatest King Scotland ever had, winning many victories and defeating great Kings. He would be the only surviving brother with a head on his shoulders and his heart would travel over numerous lands before returning home once again.

They promised him that his name would be remembered in the future. He didn't understand any of this. He just wanted to hunt wild boar, fish the river Leven and sail in his boat. He was a brave and curious boy and thought all the time about one day visiting the lions gate and seeing the huge beast for himself.

He'd never seen it but sometimes heard it during the night roaring as it was being fed. He was understandably terrified at what he might see but he had to go himself without telling anyone to overcome his fear. It was then that he decided he'd go the following day.

He awoke at first light. He slinked past the servants stoking the fire and preparing breakfast, and making sure he was careful not to be spotted leaving the house, he slipped away un-noticed down towards the river. He was excited. Today was the day he would finally see the lion.

The small wooden bridge leading over the water shook from side to side as he jumped the boards two at a time. The sun sparkled off the river surface showing hundreds of tiny baggy minnows swimming up stream away from the birds.

He was over. Now came the part he was not looking forward to; passing the Culdee monks. They were forever up early giving prayer, so he would have to be careful not to be noticed and he remained crouched, shuffling quickly through the undergrowth trying his best not to alarm the birds nesting in the reeds. Suddenly his heart skipped a beat. A monk stepped back from the waters edge, his leaky wooden bucket filled with water. They were distant baldy men who stank of that church smell. It was said they adorned baggy robes and camped alone in the quietness of places often saying prayers out loud, and when they went to the toilet they used their hands to wipe their backsides.Food was always supplied for them and every month they received money for the upkeep of the Church, paying for candles and for other things that holy people do.

Gripping his trusty sword and looking to the ground, so not to make eye contact, he tried his best to look small and invisible. He was sure the Culdee monk had seen him and bit his bottom lip in disappointment. But the monk paid no attention to him and strolled away with his water, so the boy gave out a huge sigh and bowed his head in relief.

With his path now clear he mowed through the ferns like a young deer, running for all his worth and breathing heavy like a huge ox. The sun shone bright and he was sweating due to his quick movements. Stopping for a moment he dropped his hands into the water, soaking his face and drinking the rest. The water was cold. It was always cold. Even in the height of summer the River Leven kept its icy tingle as he had experienced for himself many times with his brothers.

Now entering a small forest and disappearing between the green leaves, he was safe for the moment. No one would be able to find him now. The forest was his playground and he knew every animal and insect. Nothing could hold him back.

As he reached the outskirts of the forest he stopped and

had a good look around to make sure he knew his way back. This was also a chance to take in and enjoy his surroundings and to notice how beautiful his lands were in all their stunning beauty. The hills, river and valleys, surrounded by the wild flowers and trees were magical and it was the perfect place for a young boy to experience adventures.

He looked on. This was new ground to him and although he'd never seen this part before, moving forward was his only option. It was then he stopped to check an animal paw print he didn't recognise. It was huge. It stood on four legs and was colossal due to the deepness of the tracks in the ground. Wee Bruce placed his hand inside the paw print and opened his fingers to measure the width but before he could, a loud thundering roar frightened him, hurling him back onto the ground. He'd never heard anything like it. His stomach was knotted and he felt sick. He felt the vibration of the roar in his legs all the way up to his head and it almost deafened him.

What was this noise? What was the cause of it? He had to find out. He crawled forward on his belly for twenty feet until he came to a halt. In front of him were three men sitting on the ground facing each other, holding mighty spears and wearing long bows around their shoulders. He recognised them. They were his father's guards; three of the forty bowmen of St Sebastian. But what were they doing sitting in the middle of nowhere?

He sat crouched for fifteen minutes watching the armed soldiers talking and laughing, sometimes arguing with each other then breaking the anger with more laughter. He couldn't make out what they were saying as he was too far back and it was all just a mumble to him. He just sat there a little longer contemplating what to do next. Then for some reason the soldiers stood up, looked around and left laughing and patting each other on the back.

This was his chance to make his move. As soon as the soldiers were out of sight he stooped and scurried over to where they were sitting to have a look around. But something wasn't right. As he neared to where the soldiers sat, the ground seemed to change. All of a sudden he felt out of his depth and he could sense panic. The ground was dark and descended downwards.

As he edged closer, the dark patch of ground expanded larger and before he knew it, a hole uncovered in front of him. He stopped. The men were sitting around a hole. But why would they sit around a hole?

By remaining still and raising his chin slightly, he could examine further into the hole. What he observed dropped really deep into the ground but he still couldn't see the bottom, he had to have a closer look. The unsure sensation in his stomach began to stir strangely stronger, experiencing an uneasy feeling to turn back. He'd come this far and couldn't give up now, he really wanted to know the reason for this huge pit and the curiosity was getting the better of him, so he advanced forward a few feet.

Not venturing right to the edge he stretched his neck and slowly peeped over. With fright, a grouse hiding in the nearby forest flew out like an arrow, screaming as it passed close to his head making him cry out in alarm, forcing him to sprint back into the forest like a startled rabbit.

Almost five minutes had past before he ventured over to the pit again, his shaking and the feeling of anxiety disappeared and he was ready to have another look. Again he reached the edge. He scanned all around, searching all sides to make sure no one was around, peering back at the forest, checking there were no more grouse ready to surprise him.

One bad fright was enough and he already made his mind up that if he was forced back into the forest again he wouldn't return It was now or never. It was then that he witnessed the most spectacular sight he'd ever seen in his life. There, staring up at him with huge hypnotic eyes from the bottom of the pit was a huge beast with a massive head.

The creature eyeballed him and then seemed to bow as it dropped its head probing the ground, gnawing on a bone. Around its neck it wore a huge mane of fur and was way larger than his father's soldiers. Its paws were awesome, brandishing giant claws sharper than any blade, possessing longer legs than any wild boar he'd ever seen. It posed an awesome sight and although it portrayed a snared beast, it still shone in all its glory and majestic splendour. It paraded and flaunted its head. And what a head; far too large for its torso, with a mouth fully opened displaying heavy panting, and fangs only known in nightmares.

Sticking out from between its teeth was a tongue bigger than the size of the boy's own foot. He was mesmerised, his body was rooted to the spot as if he were a tree. He was alarmed but excited at the same time and his heart pounded constantly against his arm. The blood flow had ceased in his hand with gripping his sword so tight, but he wasn't aware of it, for he had trouble breaking away. He didn't want to leave.

So this was the beast his father warned him never to visit? This was the famous lion? An extraordinary beast and a mantle worthy of king's stature. The boy was bowled over. He was awe struck by its presence. This was the

ultimate killing machine; a beast who knew no fear; a beast who would turn from no other and a beast who would fight till the death. Its only misfortune was to be captured by man and trapped in a hole to be enjoyed like a picked rose.

At this moment, wee Bruce's heart made a connection with the lion's heart. He sensed its power, domination and resilience and would carry forward its ferocious mantle as his own.

The king of beasts stood proud, it seemed to resonate with the thoughts of the boy by discharging a huge deafening roar of approval. The thunderous shriek vibrated deeply through his being, the hair on his neck and arms standing like a church meeting, accepting its respected authority.

But there was something else about the beast that
disturbed Wee Bruce. Near to the lion lay scattered bones
arranged in piles; polished white bones, lacking flesh in
all different sizes. One particular set of bones caught his
eye. He had recalled seeing the shape before, inside an
abandoned shipwreck near Dumbarton Castle years ago. It
was a human skull. The image of a skull caught his breath,
his eyes nervously searched the pit before sighting more of
them lying in the corners; some with hair on them.

The beast was nurtured on men, and quite a lot of them
by the evidence. A closer inspection revealed piles of
hands, arms and legs. A man's torso minus its head has been
stacked away for a later snack, with an assortment of fingers
and eyeballs scattered around the pit floor. Pieces of human
meat that couldn't be recognised were massed in a ball of

flies, munching double their weight thanks to a free dinner.

Piled in the corners lay the torn blooded surcoats of past foe, their contribution and commitment to the middle ages no more. Who were these men? What part did they play in deserving this kind of end? Torn apart like a rabbit to the dogs, their screams of horror travelling un-noticed to the outside world.

The boy stepped back, and in doing so, turned to steal a final look at the beast before fading into the safety of the trees. He stopped for a few seconds, rewinding his memory to what he had witnessed, attempting to relive the image of its Herculean jaws tearing these men apart. It wasn't an image he'd want to take to bed with him. It had to be forgotten quickly or put to the back of his young mind. Slowly his head began to clear, as it was time he made his way back. His family would be searching for him and he had chanced his luck enough for one day. Although he was still in dizzy shock by the site of rotten human flesh, he was still in pure awe of the beast.

"What a magnificent animal," he thought. It surely was a King who bowed to no other.

Sneaking his way again past the eating Culdee monks, he crossed the oak bridge. Underneath, the baggy minnows bolted away at the appearance of his shadow, straight into the open mouth of a scavenging brown trout. The trout's tail splashing out of the shallow stream, made wee Bruce jump. His reaction then scattered a couple of wood pigeons in the nearby rowan tree, forcing him to jump for a second time.

As his nerves calmed he promised himself that in the future he would be valiant, immense and as proud as the lion when he grew up, and wished for his enemies to respect him as if he possessed the heart of a lion too. He also wanted to possess its strength, using the power to fight his enemies, and if ever if he was trapped, he would keep his dignity and pride as his father's animal greatly displayed. From now on he would always make sure a rampant lion was displayed on his own surcoat and armour His courage would grow immensely and he would fear nothing, not even the lion, not even the Culdee monks, not even a brown trout.

It was days like this when he felt there was a purpose in life. He began to understand there was a role for him to play in the world and if he just placed one foot in front of the other, he would eventualy get there.

Looking to the sky he did just that, with one foot in front of the other he stepped right into an abandoned, stinking cesspit!

THE END

2.
THE BOAR
by Paul V Hunter

2.

THE BOAR

Wee Bruce decided to venture into the forest. His father and close friends had departed earlier in order to check supplies at nearby Dumbarton Castle. He was bored. He was on his own. This could be the day he headed for the forest…alone. He had only foraged into the forest with his father and brothers, and was well warned never to go alone because of the danger posed by wild animals.

He'd witnessed wolves, boars and bears many a time, observing the hunt and the cleaving of meat to feed the house. To a young boy the forest can be a place of the utmost peril. Dangers lurk in every nook and cranny in such guises as poisonous plants, falling trees, birds of prey and other life threatening animals. He was aware of the dangers. He also new most fears and hazards can never be overcome without confronting the experience of being in a situation where you face being scared or challenged, counting on your reaction and survival skills to better your abilities.

For years he had been chaperoned through countless forest expeditions, knowing he couldn't be protected by others forever. He felt the time was right to go it alone It was a rite of passage, understanding he would be open to possible life threatening possibilities, but under his terms. He alone would have to deal with any given situation that arose and if need be take action to return home safe. As his father often said, "if it doesn't kill you it will make you stronger".

Before long he touched the outskirts of the forest. Proving brave enough to go it alone, this young figure was dwarfed by the massive pine trees as he trod from the safety of the familiar grasslands into the green city of branches, leaves and clotted undergrowth. Once inside he looked behind, recording his last sight of the sun and safety.

As he edged forward, the interior emerged in shadow and the decorated treetops represented umbrellas blocking the light, creating shadows and pockets of darkness everywhere. Somewhere encircling the trees he could overhear the crows chatting away, it sounded as if they were saying "Bruce, Bruce, Bruce." There was an unnerving sense he was being watched, but it continually felt that way no matter where he was.

Exploring around slowly, he focused in on every shape and possible route in his path and proceeded forward into the bushes, being careful not to trip as he trampled over the toppled trees. His sense of time had gone as he gazed back once more, noticing the safety from whence he came disappearing.

He was now in the forest alone. The aroma of the decaying vegetation was pungent and although he held his breath, he couldn't help but inhale the stinging smell. There was dampness in places underfoot and labouring to keep upright so he wouldn't fall over was tiresome, but he was pretty chuffed as he'd not tumbled yet into the mud. Then suddenly.....Wallop! He flew up into the air and crashed onto his backside like a sack of vegetables into a muddy puddle. Standing up, he brushed himself off and then..... Wallop; he was down again, in the same puddle.

Again he got onto his feet, stepping away from the watery hole. Every now and then a dried twig would snap under his weight, setting off cries from nearby blackbirds making him jump. The forest seemed to be sprouting thicker by the moment and charging through the branches was energy sapping.

Just when he thought he'd have to halt for a breather, an opening in the centre of the trees appeared, illuminated by sunlight. He decided to rest on a rock for a moment, looking around. There were no trees, instead they were substituted by massive erected stones, upright and tall, forming a circle. Someone had been here before. Placed at the foot of the stones were flowers, wrapped in bunches, standing upright against the dark grey stone giants. As he gazed upon the stones, strange markings and pictures appeared.

There were circles, lines braided and intertwined together like a woman's hair and odd images of deer and boar straddled by fearsome riders. Who could have designed these? Why were they here? He understood this was a sacred place, and not to appear as an intruder he relaxed his movements, being careful not to create any noise. He felt compelled to snap off some wild flowers, extending to the collection already there.

Enjoying the peace he sat around for a few moments soaking up the quietness; the feeling of being himself without any interference from his other brothers was bliss. He looked up through the hole in the trees, feeling the sun on his face. As he watched, two dragonflies caught his eye,

bumping into one another
and floating upwards,
the sun reflecting off
their turquoise blue bodies
and silk wings. They finally reached
a height where they gracefully became two dots
in the skyline, finally disappearing for good out and over
the green bushy canopy, blowing side to side in the wind.

He appeared to have nodded off when the noise of
snapping twigs startled him awake. Sitting up he peered
around.
"Hello," he said. "Anyone there?"
The feeling of peace he experienced earlier had somehow
disappeared, as he felt isolated and all alone. Again came
the clamour of snapping twigs. He quickly arched his head
in the direction of the noise and focused his eyes upon
the difficult greens and browns of natures camouflage. He
spotted nothing. Suddenly there was definite movement
and the noise was getting intense. Already on his feet and
sneaking forward a little, he crouched low, giving himself a
better view at the bearing he thought the movement was
coming from. Nearby birds swore as they flew off in the
opposite direction, leaving wee Bruce with a fright, forcing
his body to jump in response.

Something was stirring around him, he couldn't see who

or what it was, but whatever it was…it watched him. Not being able to notice anything began to alarm wee Bruce and he reversed backwards, hiding himself at the rear one of the great stones. Then from behind his stone protection came the noise of something forcing itself through the undergrowth, appearing to stop a few yards away, scraping its feet on the ground. Whatever it was, it vomited a snarling noise, releasing a high pitched squeal. Then silence.

The boy, never one to show fear, slowly positioned his head around the standing stone for a clearer look at this mysterious visitor. As he did his eyeballs doubled in size. Swinging his head back around and closing his eyes in disbelief, he gave homage to the sky as if to pray. He knew what it was for sure. It was his worse nightmare come true as emerging from the undergrowth was a wild boar; a full grown male.

A wild boar was capable of killing an adult man no problem. He'd noticed people around the manor house who had lived to tell the tale, wielding walking sticks and suffering missing limbs for their encounters. He remembered the boar skins on the floors and walls but they were minute compared to this beast. This wild boar was gargantuan, with tusks sticking out that could rip apart flesh and bone to pieces. Its neck was thick and its legs short and sturdy…built for the kill. A coarse wiry coat of fur protected it from the harsh weather and nature's hardships, and with a huge snotty snout twitching away, soaking up the boy's scent.

Leaning on the edge of its hooves and foaming white at the mouth, its erect tail pointed to the sky, trying to home in on its target. It sensed the boy was there but couldn't see him…yet. Wee Bruce understood that if he tried to make a run he was doomed. These animals could run as fast as a horse and since there was nowhere to run, he'd probably be killed or badly injured. He had no option but to act quickly. After running his hand against the standing stone, he felt the grooves in the artistic design and followed with his eye the carved knots climbing to the top almost like a rope. They were thick enough for his small hands to grab onto and haul himself up. Twice his foot gave way, scraping his knee against the dark grey hardness; enough to draw blood.

He ascended so quickly he seemed to forget how high he had climbed as he touched the top of this ancient monument. He sat perched like a crow riding the world, looking down at a puzzled wild boar. The creature sat there soliciting meanness, oozing more snot through frustration than a classroom full of children with head colds. He was safe for now but he couldn't remain there forever. The boar seemed to sense this. It sat motionless, staring upwards,

eyes focused on the boy.
Then the boy saw a chance.

He noted the stones
were aligned. He could
attempt to jump to each
one until he reached a small
tree close by, then climb
as high as he could out of
site, hopefully towards the
grasslands.

Jumping to the first
stone was no problem; it
was close enough to hold
on to without falling and
there was ample to grab
hold of. As he edged along so did the boar, waiting for
him, compelling him to make a mistake, desperate to make
its move. He looked the boar in the eyes, then looked to
the sky, took a deep breath and leapt into the air towards
the other stone. No sooner was he in the air, he came
crashing back down to earth striking his target. His body
battered against the solid wall as the air was thumped out of
his lungs. He'd made the first one.

The next stone was tricky. It was much farther away and
would require a good leap in reaching it. The boar was

dancing crazy, screaming and digging its hooves into the ground, forcing up dirt through the air and blasting through its snout. Through anger it would accelerate forward in sharp bursts of energy, stop, then go back to its original place. The boy spat at the boar, a ball of spit hitting it square on the head. It gave him a short feeling of triumph but that was short lived when he eyed the next jump in front of him. Standing on his toes and flexing his knees as much as he could, almost like a grasshopper, he threw himself up into the air, imitating one of his father's hunting hawks.

He seemed to be in the air for an age when gravity tugged on his body, dragging his little frame downwards. Luck seemed to be smiling upon him as one arm and leg grappled onto the ancient design and text. He'd made it again by the skin of his teeth, letting out a loud scream of relief and letting fly a few bad words at the boar in defiance. Remembering his age, he looked around for his father to hear his words, as normally the usage of them resulted in a boot up the backside, or a dizzy head from a grown-ups hand connected to the back of his skull. By this time the boar was livid. It had begun sprinting around the stones in frightening speed, screaming in all sorts of tones as if cursing wee Bruce, who let fly with another spit ball, this time, well wide of the target.

The trees were getting much closer now and with

another good jump he knew he could make it. Now it was time for him to make a choice. Landing on the following stone would certainly mean he could touch the tree with no problem; but what if he missed? Was he better reaching for the tree now? He was becoming tired and his energy was being zapped. Not spending anymore time thinking about it, he decided to go for the tree. If he missed, he could be injured by the fall and the boar would be on him, or on the other hand he could reach the safety of the trees and be gone without the boar getting a sniff.

The beast began messing with his concentration, it had dug two trenches with its front legs and was dragging its tusks along the ground, making as much noise as it could. Before the boy knew it, he was in the air gliding towards a huge branch, thick enough to take his weight and with ample twigs to get a good grip.

Everything moved in slow motion. The tree seemed to sidestep as he jumped, seeming further away than he anticipated. As he arrived at the branch, he stopped dead in mid air and without warning started to fall. He stretched out in desperation for a last gasp grabbing grasp but he plummeted like a stone towards the ground below. The slow motion had deserted him and he now obtained mega falling speed, bouncing off the ground, landing partly into the midst of a short bush. As quick as a flash he was on his feet and flying through the thick forest. His ribs hurt. After him came the horrendous screaming and squealing of the boar, feeling the heavy thumping vibration of its body contacting with the ground.

The noise of its hoofs battered on the forest floor, sounding really close at his heels. There was no possibility whatsoever of outrunning a male wild boar. He had no option but to run anyway, and keep running. His small legs hurdled a few streams as he began to recognise his surroundings. He had been here before with his father hunting, remembering just around the corner were the spike pits; deep dug hollows in the soil, covered with fern and heather to hide the trap and armed with multi sharpened spikes designed to kill animals.

As he headed in that direction he could smell the boar's rancid breath right behind him, waiting any moment for it to drive its tusks into his heavy tiring calves. Attempting to think and sprint at the same time was becoming arduous. Playing on his thoughts was the terrifying image of himself collapsing into the pit, being torn to thousands of pieces by dung painted sharp stakes, prepared mince meat for the boar.

With the boar gaining on him, wee Bruce reached the pits, and with his eyes directly looking at the ground he focused on a thin trail running between the holes. It was secure enough to bear his weight, but if he stepped on either side he was a gonner. He was betting on the boar slipping down into the pit. Gladly he would be able to stop with relief and look back at the impaled beast. He listened for the snapping of the ferns and the scream of the boar but to his horror it never came. He gave a glancing look behind, but the boar had shadowed him through the middle of the pits. What was going to stop it now?

The beast was bursting with energy and at its leisure was about to seize him. Wee Bruce's legs were driving as fast as they ever ran; it was just a matter of time before the beast caught him. Thinking his time was up, the boy's young life started to flash in front of his eyes. He thought about his mother and father, his brothers and sisters and his friends. Maybe it was through fatigue or lack of concentration but one of his legs gave way and he collapsed to the ground, smashing his face into the dirt. Everything swung into slow motion as the boy rubbed his grazed knees, he had no energy or strength to stand and he awaited its arrival and his fate. He was now aware of the boar behind him as its screams got louder and louder.

It was all over. Wee Bruce had danced his last dance; his fate now chosen by a hairy backed, snot spitting pig. He never thought in a million years he would leave this earth so young, with many things still to accomplish and experience in life. He was forever being told one day he'd be king. Now he knew for sure this wasn't going to happen.

Was it all to end in a place he adored, where he spent countless seasons exploring the animal and plant life? Was it wrong to love his surroundings and fall prey to its unpredictable hazards? It was now time to accept his fate. Taking a deep breath, he looked to the azure blue sky, realizing how simple and beautiful it was and how

he wished he had taken the time to look at it more
Two gulls flew into his line of vision, floating free of
responsibility and free from harm.

He wished he could fly, wondering what the feeling
would be like to soar on high for ages without a care in
the world. He felt sad. He never got the chance to say
goodbye to his parents. He wanted to apologise for all the
worry he had caused them and if he ever got the chance
again, he'd try to be a better son and brother. He wondered
what heaven would be like; if a multitude of singing angels
would escort him to a world of everlasting bliss or would a
gang of dark faceless demons drag him down to hell for the
years he spent stealing apples and cursing. Either way he
was going to find out soon enough. He was ready.

At last, the beast seeing its opportunity, decided to
pounce. Suddenly, there was a strange gust of wind. It was
a short burst of air followed by a swish. It flew past his left
ear and then it was gone. Strange. What was it? Whatever
it was halted the beast in its tracks. He could no longer
hear the boar. Where did it go? Why did it stop? Arriving
into his sight entered the shape of a tall man. The boy's
eyes were out of focus but as the apparition got closer
and into range he could make out the figure as one of his
fathers bodyguards. He was holding his bow, and with the
arrow in position, he aimed it over the boy's shoulder.

Standing like a statue, he beckoned the boy to remain behind him. Trembling, Wee Bruce's legs were like jelly as he stood behind the tall bowman, leaning against him to prop himself up. He then peered from behind the tall figure. Lying in front of him two feet away was the boar. Between its eyes, stuck in deep, a well made arrow halting it dead in its tracks. Its chest was still pounding, the air still sweeping through its lungs and lots more snot drooling from its snout. Its eyes were opened as if just staring straight ahead and its hind legs twitched to and fro. A split second divide was between the animal and the boy's life. Wee Bruce shielded his eyes, he'd seen enough and just wanted to go home.

For many a week in the Manor house, he slept with the boar skins off the bottom of his bed and placed them on the floor.

Through time his tired legs got stronger, his skinned knees healed very quickly and before long he was running around like his young self again with his friends. It would be a while before he ventured back into the forest alone again.

Maybe he was meant to be king one day after all.

THE END

3.
CHARITY
by Paul V Hunter

CHARITY

Wee Bruce was at the table having his usual get together dinner with his family. Every kind of food and drink you could imagine dressed the table in abundance. Something was on his mind and he wasn't hungry. He'd ventured out of his family's boundaries to experience what the world was like outside the safety of the manor house and unknown to his parents he had sneaked out days before, travelling to Luss village.

"Father, why are there poor people starving in the next village?" he asked.

The table fell silent, all his brothers and sisters looked in his direction.

"How do you know the poor people are starving in the next village?" asked his father.

He had to answer swiftly or be found out.

"I overheard two of your bodyguards talking about how needy the villagers were and they were starving and sick."

His father explained it was a similar situation all over the world and unless you were born into royalty or a noble position, life was continually going to be difficult.

He glared at his soup. "Why can't we feed them father? We have enough."

"Then why don't you give tonight's meal to the village tomorrow and do without?" asked his mother.

"Then I would go to bed hungry," he replied.

"Then you choose," she said, "You or them?"

"Typical Robert," said his brother Edward. "Always trying to turn the world upside down."

His sisters giggled and scoffed.

"I think it's very noble of you dear brother," replied Alexander.

"Hear hear," said Thomas and Nigel.

"Can I have your meal if you don't want it?" asked Margaret.

"Give me half." said Matilda laughing.

His father brought an end to the teasing, "Let him speak his mind."

Resting his spoon he spoke. "This is Scotland. Why don't we all have enough to eat and drink and be healthy, and have building wood for everyone to make proper houses?"

The table was hushed as everyone continued eating.

"You certainly heard a lot from my bodyguards didn't

you?" answered his father, "We'll have no more talk of this at the table. Let's eat."

From that moment on, the boy had decided he was journeying back to the village of Luss in the morning to have a accurate look for himself.

As sunrise welcomed in a new day he was up, out and on his way. From his shoulder hung provisions. Toothless Mary the cook had prepared him with a bag stocked with apples, bread, some fried fish and a sheep's stomach filled to store water. This was the farthest he'd ever been companionless and so far on his walk there weren't that many people around to trouble him His mother continually voiced her alarm about being robbed or even kidnapped and withheld for ransom, but he was only a boy. What mischief could there be just walking through the village?

The outskirts were identical to other places he had visited and this was the same route he'd taken days earlier. Ancient pine forests furnished the skyline and Loch Lomond pretended to

go on forever as he entered, the crows and magpies making lots of noise to warn of his presence. He reached the edge of the village and stopped at the stone marker.

There was no name. It was just a tall grey stone with animal dung plastered on top. To the edge of the stone lay a carcass of a dead cow, the bones nearly picked clean of rotting slithers of flesh and skin, and blue bottles set upon what remained. Walking past, his muddy feet squelched through a mass of black and bloody bloated boa of sludge. A little further up he pushed past an old man squatting at the edge of the dirt track. The old man's eyes wondered across the path, not noticing the small boy as he approached him.

"Good day Sir" he said in a quiet voice. No reply.

The old man continued focusing ahead, pretending as

if he wasn't there. There was no movement in his eyes and there was no indication of blinking or breathing. Wee Bruce walked on, halting every now and then, looking behind to see if the old man moved. Later, as he polished off his bread and fish, he noted on either side of the path, large wooden cages cloaked in branches and covered with hides from all sorts of animals. These were the scanty homes for most of the villagers. His heart sank for the people. The fresh grass that swelled his nostrils now mutated to stinking rotten hay and as he glanced up, one of the cages had smoke bellowing out of a hole at the top.

Inside he could hear a mother shouting and screaming in anger. Not far from the cages were little frothy streams fleeing in all directions, finally meeting up to make a reservoir about thirty feet away. It stank of urine and poo. This was the toilet. As he walked past, a hand stuck out of one of the cages, emptying a wooden bucket full of poo, splashing onto the earth beside his feet. The ground stank to high heaven.

A ten-minute walk guided him to a huge wooden shed. It was cased in three sides by wooden slats and the front was completely open, allowing him to view what lay inside. Above the opening, hung various horseshoes in all sizes and at the entrance stood a block of stone with a blacksmith's anvil resting on top.

The floor was partly cobbled and coated in an overspread of dry straw and at the back lay a wooden box topped with horse manure. The bluebottles and flies numbered in thousands. Up above on the rafters were swallows nests by the dozen, and every now and then one would swoop down so low as if attempting to touch the hair on his head. On one nest, young chicks popped out their heads to have a swift look and then popped back inside again.

Walking away from the stench, he came across two bulky barns built facing on to each other. Something inside was causing a stir, as a group of people were loitering around outside and gathered, huddling closely together like sheep.

All eyes were gazing at stalls selling a selection of local decaying fruit and vegetables and hand made farming tools. The cluster leaned as one, staring at the stalls, clothed in capes of some sort and the men wore pointed hoods hauled over their heads, almost covering their faces. The children had no shoes and were ankle deep in mud, shifting their tiny feet left to right as if straining to keep warm, holding tight onto their mother's rags as their faces were veiled from site. Most men wore untidy beards, their hands were blistered and worn with clotted black lines of dirt under the nails. They all appeared thin and the children

44

imitated broken dolls nobody wanted. The men and women had copycat forlorn expressions on their faces. It was a desperate look; a look of struggle, displaying the same deep sunken sockets underlined by deep black baggy lines. The food on the table wasn't fit for rats.

The boy wouldn't experience a worse state of living. It wasn't as if he was not catching the townsfolk at their best. This was their best. There was no more. This was a struggling rat race of a country's people, forgotten and separated by the wealthy hand of fate. As soon as the struggling masses awoke, their days began with the pain of empty bellies and cold hands, trapped inside pens fit more for animals. The locals had attitude. They were angry, desperate and weary of strangers and had every right to be. The world dealt them a bad hand, giving them a lame excuse in welcoming the inevitable comfort of an early death.

To the side of the barn lay half a horse displayed on a huge slice of wooden oak. A mean looking worker was hacking away with a short handled axe to the horse's ribs.

He yelled out that the animal was fresh and had died from disease and would take any payment. The people looked at the rotten vegetables and horsemeat with wishful thinking. Even the skinny dogs had no luck, they were being frequently kicked away, offered no titbits what so ever and barked continuously. The boy then remembered his father saying a few days earlier that there was a shortage of rabbits in the area. The locals had stalked them nearly to extinction and boar and deer were off the menu to them, they were royal meats and were protected by law.

The rivers were swollen of fish but the locals had been raised up on this diet all their lives and were sick to the back teeth of fish meat. He glanced over to the river bank, lined in rank upon the bank were men and women, gawping into the water.

Nobody was fishing. Nobody cared. Half sunken into the gravel, flaunted dead bloated sheep; their stinking bodies making that part of the river un-usable and the stench of death filled the air with the recognisable smell of rotten flesh. Hoards of the living dead sat around in bundles, some singing Gaelic songs of their ancestors, some praying out aloud to why God was ignoring their pleas. The assemblages were soul destroying to the eye, they queued continually, fighting amongst themselves in finding the key to death's door to finally end their living hell of misery

As he wandered through the local people, the boy was conscious that someone was watching him. Turning around he caught eyes with a huge bald man, whose face was secreted in scars and fronted with a bruised broken nose...

"By the name of St. Serf that's a Bruce!" he screamed. "That's a Bruce!" Wee Bruce stopped and looked at the man.

The bald man screamed again and pointed his finger, "He's a Bruce boy, he's worth a fortune and he's on his own. Stop him!"

Most people failed to react to his screams, they had heard screams a million times through desperation and loss and they were immune to them. With his heart almost leaping out of his mouth, his legs began to flee without him thinking about it. He had to get out of there rapidly. The warning from his mother was now repeating itself in his head. He was in danger.

Abandoning his side bag and shaking with fear, he panicked as his legs felt heavy filled with invisible water, running away towards the direction of home. A lot of shouting pursued him from behind, as more people joined in on the chase, making his legs feel even heavier to move. Running through a barn to escape, he came upon a shed, squeezing through a gap in the broken wood he disappeared out the back towards the marshes and woods.

This would give him a head start away from the advancing villagers. As he headed for home, his short cut took him across a field of graves, the upturned piece of lifeless land looked like a giant hedgehog, hundreds of wooden crosses imitating the small animal's spikes. The crosses were crude, any two pieces of stick tied together with whatever they could get their hands on. One such home made effort was twined by the occupants own hair tied in rope-like fashion. Most of the graves were small, some occupied by wailing mothers, shattered at their heart breaking loss. New visitors to the site and bereft of digging tools, used their bare hands, creating shallow ditches in which they placed forever sleeping young ones clothed in their everyday peasant rags. Wee Bruce had never seen such tragedy.

Fearing an ambush up ahead he decided to head for the swamps and lay low for a while. An hour had past, light was fading and he now found himself waist deep in the marsh. He was beginning to lose the feeling in his legs. The water was very cold as he tucked his hands under his armpits trying to keep warm. It wasn't working. By now he was shivering uncontrollably and had to exit the water before it was too late. Immediately after walking on dry firm ground he could feel the heat trying to enter his body. He was so chilled his mind wondered. Is this how the other children in the village felt, being so cold and hungry at night they couldn't sleep? How could they survive and why were these countless deaths never brought up back home?

On the other side of the water the bald man and his cronies continued their hunt for him, searching every blade of grass for their possible money earner. He would have to stay hidden until he reached the safety of his own lands. He thought hard. If he could make it to the old stone bridge half way across the hill, he'd have a decent chance of losing them in his forest.

It was then he had another thought; surely his mother and father would realize he was missing by now? After running non-stop, he slowed down to rid the painful knot in his side. By now, in matching his damp bottom half, his top half was wet too. He was sweating like crazy, using his fingers to shift the burning salty sweat from his eyes.

His small frame ached and his calf's cramped numerous times before he reached the bridge out of breath. From under the old farmers bridge he lifted his mouth upwards to catch the cascading droplets of water, and swallowed as much as he possibly could without choking. He was half way home and he felt better already.

His happiness was short lived as he heard voices close by. Sneaking out from under the bridge he catapulted himself into a ditch, landing on soft cattle dung. It was a fresh one, a lovely green soft one spilled into his eyes, sticking to his eyebrows, running up his nose and down through his mouth, finally resting on his tongue. He gagged.

Covering himself with fallen branches, he controlled his breathing so not even a mouse could hear him. The voices grew louder, stopping to a halt ten feet away from him. He could make out two dark figures perching on top of the bridge and two dark figures under the bridge.
"He can't be far." said a voice, "Don't worry we'll get him."
"I'm going to skin the little pig when I get hold of him." said another. One of the rogues picked up a heavy rock.
"If he were here now I'd crack his head open with this," smashing the rock to the ground, missing the boy by inches.

Wee Bruce then listened carefully as the men spoke of their plot to capture him dead or alive, planning in getting

close to his family and setting fire to the barns, stealing
cattle and riding away on the horses. His dung filled ears
couldn't believe what he was hearing. After talking through
their organised plan, the men left, sprinting by mistake into
the darkness, disappearing deep into the marshes. In the
coldness could be heard the noise of their screaming , as
they fell into the chilling water. It was difficult controlling
his laughter, as he relished the idea of the bald man and his
friends being lost in the dark and soaking wet. No sooner
had the men left, they re-appeared again, resting at the
bridge. They could hardly speak as their teeth chattered
from the icy loch, trying their best in uttering swear words,
but with no success.

"Let's just go back," said one of the friends, "He's not worth it."
"Good idea," said another, "He probably drowned, the little
weasel."

"Aye," said the bald man, "I've made a mistake, he wasn't a Bruce boy. It was a bit much to think a royal brat would ever think of visiting our village anyway."

They left dripping, shivering and miserable at their gamble in tasting wealth.

Wee Bruce rested ten minutes to make sure they were gone, and then jumped up onto his feet and commenced running again. This time he refused to stop for the knots in his side, instead he ran without a rest. As he struck home the dogs were barking and candles and torches were burning all over the manor house. He'd finally made it back safe, and as he sneaked around, there was a hive of activity with men at arms running everywhere combing around the edge of the river.

His legs were in pain from the walking so he headed straight for the bedroom. Once inside, he covered himself in warm furs and sank off to sleep behind the room chair. A lit candle and shouting aroused him with a relieved looking father staring down on him.

"Where have you been?" he asked, "We've searched everywhere for you."

"I've not been anywhere father, I fell asleep here hours ago." replied the tired boy.

His father, picked him up and after putting him into bed, left the chamber and headed downstairs shouting, "Its ok he's here! He's here! No need to worry everyone, he's ok, he fell asleep behind the chair, call the guards off."

"Idiot," shouted his brother Nigel.

"Little fool," shouted his sister Mary, "scaring us all to death."

"That's enough," came back his mothers voice, "He's safe, that's all that matters."

As calmness returned, he was back in the safety and comfort of his own bed, his surroundings were his own and a long way from any danger for the time being.

A few hours lapsed and all was quiet. A full moon shone through the window and although he was overtired, he couldn't sleep. The images of the locals suffering was hard to swallow. It wasn't something he could forget about in a hurry.

He was surprised when the door opened and in walked his father with candle in hand.

"How are you feeling son?"

"I'm alright father, a little cold," he replied.

His father tucked him in. "Did you find what you were looking for?"

A tear ran down his cheek, "They're starving father. The children are small and skinny with nothing to eat and are suffering, but how did you know where I was?"

His father blew out the candle. "Because you're my son.

Now get to sleep and less of this worrying."

His father left the room. The door closed then opened again. "Before your mother sees you in the morning make sure you wash, you stink of cow dung."

Before going to sleep, he kneeled at the bottom of his bed and prayed for help and guidance for the unfortunate villagers who were suffering. He even said a prayer of forgiveness for the men who hunted him earlier; He understood their plight.

When morning eventually arrived, wee Bruce was awoken by the racket of horse and carts close to the manor house. Peeping through the wooden shutters he observed his father giving orders to his workers who were stocking up the carts with deer carcasses, fruit, vegetables and dry wooden boards. "Make sure you go straight to Luss," he ordered, "Hand them out to everyone, and when you return I'll give you more."

His father was dispatching food and building boards to the needy in the village. Wee Bruce watched, as the convoy of food wagons disappeared over the hill. The villagers might have been poor and famished but they were his people too.

THE END

4.
THE TOURNAMENT
by Paul V Hunter

4. THE TOURNAMENT

Wee Bruce had just returned from spending the night at Dalreoch. It was a short ride from the manor house, taking half an hour to get there by horse and cart. He didn't get much sleep as he was too excited at the prospect of what was ahead and it thrilled him to pieces being back home.

It was pavilion day. People from all over the country would show up in their fine clothes, horses and armour to participate in the annual jousting tournament. It was also a chance for him to disappear into the crowd and have a nosey around. There would be a huge gathering of people with different accents, enough to number a small army and enough food to feed ten small armies. If there was something this boy loved it was food.

Flags caught his eye as the wind battered about the different banners, making them flutter with pride. The hot sun glistened off the flour-white robes and surcoats of the pages as they ran around like dogs after their masters, dancing to the sound of the horn blowers stretching their lips. The women and children were fenced in according to status and for safety from falling horses. Below them were the blacksmiths bellowing hot steam as they worked on the horses metal shoes. But there was a darker side to the tournament. Sometimes if the crowd were lucky a jousting knight would be thrown from his horse, snapping his lance as he fell. The pages in their clean clothing would be smothered in spilt blood and there would be screams of horror from the ladies stand, always ending in some princess fainting and being escorted from the field.

He dreamt of himself taking part one day and winning the tournament, becoming the strongest knight in all the land; his name being mentioned in far away lands, echoing his exploits. Little did he know that today he would have some influence between the sporting knights and their outcome. He easily slipped away from his minders, keeping his head down as he dropped down low.

His favourite place was under one of the numerous huge oak tables, where on top was placed an assortment of weaponry and armour. It was always soft with a new covering of smelly fresh straw and was great to stretch out on. Covering the whole tabletop and touching the grass below was a thick purple tablecloth with a yellow shield and red lion sewn into the middle. The heat from under the table was stifling and every now and then he would get a whiff of fresh cut timber and the smell of fresh baked bread. They were the nice smells.

There was also the stench of polished armour, the over scented ladies soaked in oil from the Far East and of course… horse dung. The smell didn't come from the horses but from the pages shoes and leggings as they ran behind the animals with baskets, catching the slop before it spoiled the grass.

Apart from this it was the perfect place to hide. Suddenly there was a fanfare of off-tune trumpets and the tournament was about to begin. The horses seemed to sense the tension as a few of them screeched into the air, outdone by a huge roar of applause coming from the crowd. For a split second the heralds and pages took

their eyes off the table, failing to notice something falling onto the ground next to wee Bruce, making him turn his head immediately. Whatever the object was, half of it was under the table and without thinking, his little hand snatched at it, sitting it between his legs. At the same time he re-coiled his hand back as something sharp cut into his finger releasing a small flow of blood. It was a spur.

It was no ordinary spur. It shone like gold and was strapped together with brand new oiled leather. He was keeping this. Without cutting himself again it was carefully wrapped in a piece of cloth and placed into a small leather pouch that hung around his shoulder. This was something special to show his friends later. He then crawled on his hands and knees towards the end of the table and lifting the edge of the decorated purple cloth, he had the perfect vantage point to observe the knights as they prepared for battle. His belly rumbled. Into his vision came a cloud of flies around the countless cooked meats roasting on the spits, reminding him that he had no breakfast this morning.

About twenty feet away, a page received a beating for not performing his duties properly and a group of young children ran past him trying to hit a dragonfly with sticks.

Things were hotting up nicely and he sensed this was going to be a special day. Farther away important men were bowing towards the ladies and fat men were trying to squeeze into thin armour. From behind a wooden army of hanging chainmail there was, however, one knight dressed in black armour who always stood out.

There seemed to be a feeling of dislike towards him from most people and this knight didn't care. The boy knew his father didn't like the black knight as he heard him telling his mother in not-so-many words. Again, this mysterious annoying champion, in all his splendour, would stand out as the man to beat in this tournament. As his horse sweated in the heat he gulped down a goblet of drink, half of it running down his black pointy beard.

Then without safety for anyone he threw the goblet into the crowd, just missing the Queen of Norway's head. There wasn't even a hint of an apology. He was a horrible man. He was immense and his armour was dark and dull, giving off no shine. On his chest was a red shield with three yellow lions matching his hand-held shield and the same mixture of a coloured plume expanded out of his great helmet.

By now the sun felt as if it was getting warmer and the smell of over heated, baked rowan trees filled the air. Every now and then there was a sharp welcome breeze from the river Leven, catching the ladies headdresses, covering their faces and orchestrating a huge laugh.

It was then that he noticed the black knight was wearing one golden spur on his right foot. He screamed at his helpers as they scurried around looking for the lost one. One herald received a thump on his head from a heavy hammer called a mace, felling him to the ground. Without looking, the boy groped the inside of his pouch, making sure he still had the other one safely hidden. He had no intentions of giving it back to this rude giant of an ape. Anyway, he didn't steal it…he found it. By this time the black knight was screaming obscenities and was hurriedly presented by another spur; a different colour, which was fastened to his other foot.

A few seconds later he dropped his helmet visor over his face and kicking his horse, moved into position for his first challenger. Without having time to think and with the horse's hooves hammering on the soil like thunder in anticipation, the trumpets sounded and two knights were on their way towards each other with speed. As the horsemen clashed, he had to cover his ears to stop the pain as a loud crack of metal and snapping wood rung out across the surrounding area.

A sickening groan informed him that the black knight's opponent had come off second best and lay motionless in

a heap on the ground. His pages ran to his aid, armed with herbs and ointments. It didn't look good.

A herald looked across to the main stand and motioned his finger across his neck. This meant he was badly injured and his challenge was over. Wee Bruce sat under the table staring at nothing, trying to take in what had just occurred. Just then the trumpets sounded again and the black knight was powering towards another chivalrous opponent who fancied his chances. The boy returned to his position just in time to see another brave knight dressed in blue, fly fifteen feet into the air and land with a crash of broken armour. It didn't finish there. The black knight had now positioned himself facing the main pavilion. Lifting his visor he fired abuse at the direction of the boy's father and mother. Again this was something he practised year after year.

"Are there no men in Scotland. Must I keep fighting cowards of this country who know I am un-defeated? Why don't you arm a sheep it might have a better chance?"

In keeping the peace, his parents said nothing and the cruel knight returned to his corner, spitting on the ground as he returned. The boy dived under the table. He wasn't happy the way his parents had been treated. Was there no one to stop this mad man? A massive bout of cheering summoned him into having another look, witnessing the entrance of a local hero. He was Sir William, Earl of Lennox, a young man in his twenties and winner of many hand-to-hand combat tournaments. If anyone had a chance of defeating the horrible black knight it was William.

He knew William, as the Earl of Lennox was present the day he learned to swim. He had visited the manor house on several occasions and was a well-mannered friend of the family. The boy noticed his father's chest swell; as he also knew William was a champion in the making.

The black knight laughed. "Is this it? You send a skinny boy to do a man's work? I shall never be defeated and this Scotland will always lose. "One day this land will belong to my country…onward!"

The trumpet blasted and the crowd were on their feet, hopes high for the young Earl of Lennox. His smaller but fitter horse galloped towards this huge knight, rearing its front legs as it left the starting position. He was the last hope. This time the excited boy wasn't going to cover his ears or shut his eyes. It was then the two horses screamed and clashed with an enormous thud. The crowd was silent.

Everything seemed to move in slow motion. The moment seemed to last forever until the silence was broken by the noise of a suit of armour as it hit the middle rail and collapsed on the ground. It wasn't the result everyone wanted to see. It was turning out to be a bad day. The black knight returned to his starting position and re-armed himself with a new lance.
"Is there no-one else?" he shouted.

By tournament law a knight had to win three jousts to obtain the title of champion and it was looking bad on the house of Bruce if no one came forward to accept the challenge. All the people in the main stand turned their heads looking for a challenger and it was beginning to look as though the tournament was over when a huge roar came from the common people spectators, who had positioned themselves at the other side of the river Leven. The young Earl of Lennox had remounted and was arming himself once more in readiness for the next round. He was not finished yet. Just a few seconds on the saddle and he was off, charging up wind against his foe, failing to clean spilled blood which decorated his chest armour with a red design. Bang!

Princesses screamed, fainting on the spot. Everyone rose to their feet as all eyes focused on the centre of the pavilion. Both riders seemed to wobble with the impact, but as they broke away from each other the young Earl of Lennox slipped from his horse once more onto the ground landing on his behind. The black knight dropped his lance and leaned heavily to one side but managed to correct himself in time and made it to the other end. Once again cheers went up as young William climbed his mount and gripped another lance. This time blood rained from his mouthpiece.

"This lad will not stop until he loses his life. I fear for him." said wee Bruce's father.

It was then the boy realized something was different. The black knight was starting from beside his table. The knight's horse was so close he could touch it. He carefully lifted the purple cloth to have a closer look. The horse's feet were very big and hairy with massive shiny shoes. They were broader than his two hands put together as he lifted the tablecloth even higher revealing long black oiled legs that went on forever stamping on the soil, sending stones and grit into the air. Lucky for the boy he was fast enough to duck as a small flying stone could have taken his eye out.

The tablecloth edged even higher and he spied a golden spur just like the one he had in his pouch, wrapped around a huge black armoured foot. It was the black knight all right. His massive legs and thighs clutched to the sides of his mount, and running down from inside the saddle was his ride's milk-white stinking sweat. This horse was an enormous beast; a beautifully stunning and healthy animal.

Looking up he popped his head outside for a better look. This time he got a proper close up of the black knight who didn't notice him underneath. He was mean looking. A huge single black centipede of an eyebrow covered his whole forehead. His eyes, staring, sunk deep into his head, giving the appearance of madness and mischief. There was no colour except the white of his eyeballs; so white they highlighted every red vein. His hair and beard were blacker than bland black, giving off a glossy look. He thought and wondered maybe this is why he was called the black knight.

His dark hair didn't stop there…long arrow-like strands of hair stuck out from inside his nostrils, becoming part of his moustache. A black space separated his huge front teeth and as he spoke his tongue seemed too big for his mouth as if imitating a lizard. Huge spits of saliva filled the air as he breathed with two white lines filling the edges of his mouth and his voice was heavy and vibrated just like his father's first thing in the morning. He was an ugly brute giant of a man. From nowhere a cold shiver ran over the young boy's whole body as the hairs on his arms and neck stood to attention. He felt sick.

The black knight had caught his eye and was staring through him. For an endless time both their gazes were fixed on each other. It could only have been a few seconds but was enough for him to sense the hatred and evil in this man. Without warning and from between the dark space of huge front teeth, was fired a missile ball of spit in the boy's direction. Splat! The target area hit was his shoulder and neck. No one had ever spat on wee Bruce, not even his own friends…even when they were playing.

He felt disgusted and angry. Grabbing the edge of the

table cloth, and wiping off as much sticky spit as he could he again looked at the black knight, who after giving a hint of a smile, blocked one nostril with one gauntlet finger and emptied his other nostril with an exploding blow of snot. "It's time to finish off this young Lennox. Let's get this over with." said the black knight.

Wee Bruce was scared. William was his friend and didn't want anything bad happening to him. He had to do something quick but what could he do? The trumpet sounded for action and the shout of "onward" came from the black knight. If the boy was going to do something it had to be now. Without realising, his hand was in his pouch holding onto his spur. He looked at it. Thinking, he concentrated really hard.

"Stick it onto the horses tail." said a girls voice next to him under the table.

The boy jumped back about three feet with fright. It was Elizabeth Murray. But Elizabeth Murray died a year earlier, drowning in the 'Sauny Hole' area of the River Leven. Her appearance was pitiful. Her lovely brown hair was now matted, hanging forward over her pale, almost white complexion. Her eyes were dark and she'd lost the sparkle she used to carry in those beautiful brown eyes of hers.

"I thought you'd drowned," he said.

"Stick the spur onto the horses tail." said Elizabeth.

"But I thought you drowned!" he repeated.

In a calm voice she replied, "Stick the spur onto the horses tail now Robert."

Grabbing the spur, he flung his arm outwards and lost his hand in the mangle of long black horsehair. The spur was so sharp it clasped onto the tail like a bag of worms on a fishing hook. A few seconds later the horse and rider were in full gallop.

He turned around to Elizabeth "That was close." he added, but Elizabeth was gone. He rested his chin on his chest. "I wont forget you Elizabeth and I'll pray for you. I miss you."

His thoughts were broken when a screaming horse broke his concentration. This time he stood up from under the table in full view as all eyes were on the middle of the pavilion. This was it. The black knight's horse kicked its hind legs all the way up as its rider had difficulty holding on. For a moment the four legged beastie slowed to kick the air with its front legs, then after composing itself, began to pick up speed again. By this time the black knight had lost all patience and began sticking his spurs deep into the horse's side causing it to turn sideways. The two horses reached each other and clashed with an almighty clatter. This time the black knight was off balance.

His lance missed the Earl of Lennox by a mile and he was half off his saddle by the time he reached him. Young William however was in full stride, lance straight and determined to win. During the clash, the Earl's lance managed to imbed itself under the armour close to the black knight's armpit. There was no way he would escape this time.

The impact was so fierce that the lance came through the other side, knocking the black knight flying into the air. He somersaulted a few times to the delight of the crowd and landed hard on his head as he continued to bounce and roll for a good twelve feet. As the roly-poly came to a stop he sat up, took his helmet off, looked around the pavilion and fell back flat on his back. He was finished. His aids didn't bother rushing to his side, they all stood around laughing their heads off.

Young William was the champion. Well-wishers surrounded him and cheering admirers shouted praises at him, touching his armour with their hands. He was the new hero. Wee Bruce's mother stood applauding, as did many others and his father punched the air with delight.

No one seemed to notice, but away in the distance running and kicking between the openings to the forest was a black horse, trying to shake off a golden spur from its tail. The boy laughed.

The day couldn't have ended any better than this. The Earl of Lennox was the champion and the black knight was defeated, carried off the field with his reputation in tatters. He wouldn't be back for a long time. By now the smell of cooked meat and warm honey waffed up his nose, his appetite had grown and boy was he hungry. It was then the peace was broken…

"Robert!!" Yelled a voice from the main stand. His father had spotted him. He'd been caught. No dinner for him.

THE END

5.
COIN
by Paul V Hunter

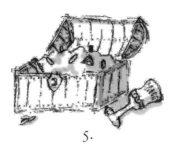

5.

COIN

Walking along a steep slippery embankment minding his own business, wee Bruce lost his balance and tumbled head first down the soaking rotten wild vegetation. Fighting his losing battle against gravity, he struggled to hold onto the wet grasses, allowing the dark brown earth to fill up the spaces behind his fingernails as he grappled on for sheer life. As his body finally touched down at the bottom lowermost hard ground, the pain in his backside reminded him that no trouser material had survived the vertical journey and his buttock skin stung owing to every known nettle clinging onto him on the way down.

At the bottom awaited his welcoming party in the form of a huge shell duck and her ducklings. Sipping water at the base of the ridge, the mother duck didn't seem too impressed with the boy's subtle entrance. It wagged its tail in disapproval and waddled off farther down the stream to a spot void of flying somersaulting young boys. With a loud quack, she situated herself and young family into the nearest pool of water and splashed down, tried her best to retrieve peace and quiet.

He looked around. He was disappointed he let himself fall. Apart from his eyeballs there wasn't a part of him that escaped the muddy helter-skelter ride. He was dirty from head to toe. Then something glittering caught the youngster's eyes. From his accidental vantage point, he spotted a perfect round shape of shining gold from under a few inches of fresh clear hill water.

Leaning forward onto his knees he plucked the object from the nipping cold water and examined it as the water ran off in quick speed. As it mixed together with his dirty black fingernails it turned to mud, forcing the wet soil to run down his sleeves. He'd never seen anything like it. It was beautiful. It was heavy. It was a coin.

Looking rather large nestled in the palm of his hand, the shiny burnished metal glowed with brilliance, its overwhelming radiant appearance was mesmerising and hypnotic and the more he looked at it the more he saw.

A picture appeared of two men in chainmail armour sharing a single horse, on the reverse side stood an image of Dumbarton Castle, surrounded by twelve decorated shields. He tucked it into a tight pocket at his hip and began the long wet muddy journey home.

The boy sat at the dinner table and listened with his eyes to the floor, as his parents tore into him about arriving home drenched in mud for the second day running. "You could have injured yourself," shouted his father. His mother didn't hold back her anger. "You won't be happy till you bring home a disease and pass it onto everyone."

His father slammed the table with his fist. "There's nothing up there I've told you before…why can't you just play in the barn with your brothers?" He scratched his head in frustration and came to a decision. "That's it, there's only one thing we can do."

Wee Bruce carefully placed the coin on the table, replacing his hands, palms down onto his knees. His father's eyes practically jumped out of his head. "What's that?" he asked.

The boy explained how he found it, saying he only fell in the mud when he tried to retrieve it. His father stood up, knocking his chair to the ground and stood motionless staring at the coin. His mother stared at his father. "Go outside and play, boy." he said.

"What?" replied his mother.

He pointed to the door. "Go now son, go outside. I'll speak to you another time about dirty clothes".

From outside wee Bruce could hear his parents talking but couldn't make anything out of the murmuring. There were no raised voices, only a low toned conversation that seemed to last for ages with endless moments of pregnant pauses. It was obvious the coin had some sort of effect by his father's reaction and he now wondered if it was the right decision showing it to them.

Later on in the evening a rider was dispatched from the manor house. Usually when this occurred something really serious was going on. As the sleepless nights passed he spent hours staring at the huge moon, it seemed bigger than normal. A creamy white haze surrounded it making it hard to make out the detail on this lunar curiosity.

As normal he didn't remember dropping off to sleep and as first light broke, the boy was summoned to his fathers quarters to speak in private. His father wanted to know exactly where the boy had found the coin and was made to promise not to ask any questions about what he had found; not even to his own brothers and sisters. With this in mind, he retraced his steps in his head, describing the area and the exact spot of his golden find.

As the story goes; before wee Bruce was born, travelling fighting holy warriors called the Knights Templar were forced to come to Scotland for protection against their enemies. With them they brought riches beyond imagination from the far east in the shape of gold, silver and precious jewels. Unfortunately, their treasures were hidden never to be found and the location was never disclosed to anyone except a selected few. For years all over Scotland, men have spent their lives hunting down these life changing riches but to no avail and due to lack of evidence or finds of treasure. The story was finally put down to ancient folklore and legend. Old mother Black, the local storyteller, said the treasure was hidden in the local area but nobody ever listened to her visions as she was considered mad.

"Look by the water," she would often shout at passers bye, but no-one would pay any attention to a near deaf old wrinkly woman with one eye.

Things definitely changed around the Manor house

after the boys discovery, there was an air of excitement and euphoria never felt before as everyone around the Cardross lands were talking about treasure. Visitors to the Manor house would come and go and there would be loud arguments and the slamming of doors and other times an eerie silence.

Throughout the coming weeks wee Bruce kept his promise to his father. It was hard keeping it secret but he gave his word and was sticking to it. There was one advantage to it however and the skip in his step proved it, his parents never mentioned his muddy clothes again. One particular morning at the dinner table, his brothers poked fun at the so-called gold discovery, often laughing it off as mere stories of fantasy and no gold was ever found in the first place. From across the table his mother would give him a sneaky stare and his father would wink to reassure him not to react to their taunts and teasing. But keeping his secret was becoming arduous and the challenge of keeping quiet was becoming more difficult as the days passed.

He had to get away from it all before he exploded with frustration, so come the following morning, he decided to return to the place where he'd found the gold piece and search the area.

It didn't take too long before he arrived at the point where he lost his footing. Making sure not to repeat the

same backside-hurting mistake, he peaked over the edge
to find an easier spot to descend. In doing so, he again
lost his balance and as before tumbled head first down
the gorge. Reaching the bottom he couldn't believe he
was top to toe in mud again and all he could think of
was his parents faces as he stood there caked in more dirt.
Finding the exact spot was no problem, he'd left footprints
in the uncovered sand next to the stream and it was just
a matter of following them. But as he moved onwards he
noticed much larger footprints, his tracking skills saw a
group of grown-ups were there and had stopped, searching
for something.

During his own search
he glanced around the
stream next to him, but
saw nothing that looked
like gold or coins, so he
continued farther up
the water and stopped
at a sharp bend in
the stream's path. Red
sandstone walls twelve
foot tall stood out
on the far side of the
embankment, decorated

with clumps of wild grasses. The grass reminded him of his fathers hair sticking out his ears, not a pretty sight when you're eating your dinner. He stopped for a moment and wondered if there was really templar Knights gold and if he were one, where would he hide the treasure. He sat down on a stone and closed his eyes. Then concentrating really hard he tried to make thinking contact with the spirit of nature.

Speaking inside his head, he asked the ancient spirits of Scotland if they could help him find the lost treasure of the templar Knights. It wasn't long before he experienced strange physical happenings. His body felt really light and the ground under him became very soft like sponge, and just to make sure he wasn't just sinking into the mud he opened one eye. Relieved that the ground was still solid, he closed his eyes again and resumed contact with the invisible powers of the forest.

It was then things got really freaky. A shadowy darkness appeared over him, forcing him to open his eyes and look up. What he saw was unbelievable. A vanguard of butterflies cloaked the skies with a multitude of floating wonder and colour reflecting against the suns rays. A freak of nature orchestrated and driven by the earth's gravitational pull, mapped out each single passage for these inspirational fluttering fancies, a gentle breeze to the left and a feint to the right they journeyed as floating summer snowflakes searching out the lands below, bestowing this flower-drift upon the dry swollen forest with pulsating buds. Each germinated shoot was besieged and besotted by rivals of natures design, succumbing to overwhelming coordinated and marauding flying small copper butterflies. Squadrons of Red Admirals and Painted ladies homed in on their targets of the delightful fragrance of the honeysuckle and the red rich purple thistles and attractive clovers.

Above them in queues, hovered sky touching towers of clouded yellows, holly blues and tortoiseshells waiting their turn, even the larger species paused to wait as size in the butterfly world had no bearing…all were equal. The world for now was as thin as paper and light as the breeze that delivered them. It was a wonderful spectacle.

Catching his eye, the boy watched a single unique butterfly float up the red sandstone, coming to a stop on a clump of hanging wild grass. It perched itself upon a grass stalk and preceded with a display of dancing and criss-crossing of its antenna. If ever there was a sign to follow this was it. Scaling the wall was hard work because of the wetness of the boy's clothes.

Every now and then his feet would slip from their hold and his fingers would give way of their grip, but this didn't deter him, he was stubborn and on a mission of real importance. As he reached closer to his target the butterfly perched itself on his nose and remained dead still. His nose totally tickled with tingle and his natural instinct was to scratch it, but hanging twelve feet off a rock by his finger tips and with a solid ground to fall on, he wasn't ever going to let go. The grassy clump was well rooted into the rock so the boy held onto it, using it as leverage to pull himself upwards and inwards. The grass clung onto the inside of a huge crack and from outside looking in, it opened up enough for his small figure to squeeze through.

Getting in between the crack was easier than he thought as he wriggled like a worm, managing to push himself inside inch by inch. Outside on the ground mother duck arrived in time to witness the boy's feet disappear into the rock, she shook her tail feathers in disapproval and waddled on with her ducklings in tow.

His whole body was in. The space inside sank in about
ten feet and came to a dead end. Then his knee sank into
something horrid, stopping him in his tracks and releasing
hundreds of blue bottle flies. It was the remains of a dead
mouse surrounded by mountains of bird droppings. The
blue bottles caused wee Bruce a slight panic as they flew
everywhere, into his eyes and his hair and around his
mouth, making him lash out with both hands to swat them
away.

As his eyes accustomed to the interior darkness, light
coloured objects at the rear of the den stood out. He then
crawled on his hands and knees to investigate and stopped
as his hand felt a soft sack material with very hard and
solid objects inside. By now his heart was beating rapid and
beads of sweat from climbing and lack of air in the den ran
down his face.

The sacks were fastened by cord, tied around the top
and were released effortlessly as he turned it upside down,
tipping its contents over the floor.

He couldn't believe it. Mountins of coins spilled
beneath his feet, just like the one he'd found outside. He
picked them up in both hands and let them fall just to
observe the gold shine in front of his eyes. He was
surrounded by ruby's, diamonds, necklaces, rings, holy

books encased in gold frames, crosses decorated in gold and silver and spangled with red stones. Bags of lined pearls were sat upon bags of rectangular gold cut ingots sat upon bags of silver and copper cut ingots. Sacks that couldn't budge by the excess weight were filled to the rim with an array of different sizes and weights of coins.

Gold handled procession swords and silver laden axes were stacked up against one side, adorned with enough decorated jewels, rendering them too heavy and only manageable for a strong man. Intricate silver daggers designed by both Christian and Muslims were laid flat and trenched in at the rear of the den, and on top, covered by a blanket of heavily gold laden wristlets, fastened by rubies mounted on silver symbolic images of the sun. There were various crowns soaked in precious metals, strewn across the floor. These once adored and highly venerated objects of antiquity once sat on the heads of the worlds highest nobles, now discarded on the dusty floor like old shoes.

Amongst the unusual objects in the den were wooden elephants, each of the their toes gilded and huge trunks, too big for their bodies, dressed in glittering diamonds. A favourite of wee Bruce was a small copper crowned ebony head of a Moorish King, it's eyes were replaced by two huge green emeralds and seemed to stare at him as the light strained through the crack from outside, reflecting upon them and bringing them to life. He sat a crown upon his head and placed on his fingers and thumbs heavy finger rings. He had performed a self crowning coronation and although the boy was surrounded by all the wealth imaginable he felt nothing clothed in material luxury.

He felt more for his own wooden sword, he'd designed and carved it himself from an old dying yew tree at Loch Lomond and it was the most precious thing he possessed. Then, because his focus had been partially blinded by his treasure find, he remembered something…the butterfly was still perched upon his nose. It had sat motionless the whole time and the tickling had now stopped. He had crowned himself King of the world with a butterfly on his nose and wondered if he was now the King of the butterflies.

He gently removed the insect onto the back of his hand and leaned forward towards the entrance. At first the delicate beauty didn't want to go, so with a little gentle persuasion it stepped effortlessly into the air, disappearing out into the light and out of sight.

Now wee Bruce was left with an important issue at hand… disclosing his discovery. He understood it was impossible to carry the treasure trove back with him, and placing a small golden cross in his hip pocket he about turned and crawled towards the exit. The cross was beautiful, enough to prove his find to his father and verify his fantastic discovery.

The boy didn't make a grand entrance arriving home, instead he kept it low key and headed straight for his father's chamber, his little heart beating with excitement.

His knuckles just about made contact with his fathers oak chamber door, when the sound of his stern voice stopped him in his tracks. Inside, his deep voice was raised and the boy could hear the tension and anger in his arguing, as objects began making contact with the surrounding walls, smashing again as they hit the floor. Now was not a good time to tell his father abut his finds, and as he turned to leave, his father screamed that he wished the boy had never found the coin. Wee Bruce's heart sank. He decided to go to his room and with his fathers comments still fresh in his memory he quickly dropped off to sleep.

He dreamed. The villagers had built a ladder from fallen trees and had gained entry to the secret den. They were throwing coins and treasure down below, showering the awaiting crowds with multiple gold and silver gifts. It was a feeding frenzy, everyone was screaming and fighting, trying to pack as many coins into their pockets as they could. Wee Bruce screamed at them to keep the secret and to put the treasure back but no sound came out his mouth and all was in vain.

Pack horses transported all the booty back to the village as a multitude of bandits and thieves danced and celebrated in their discovery. Once again, the boy begged the raiders not to take the fortune but was pushed to the ground by a greedy man eating coins and sporting a beard fill of jewels.

His mother and father shook their heads with disappointment, staring in disbelief at him wrapped in mud. Dirty ear trees stretched out their branches, with dead diseased mice covered in blue bottles hanging like earrings. The stream below was totally covered with an armada of floppy fallen butterflies, their stunning colours washing off, causing the water to run in yellows, blues, reds and whites.

The boy opened his eyes. He sat up in bed and was confused about his bad dream He always felt different after a wee sleep, and already made his mind up to return to his rich den high up in the red sandstone. Before leaving, he wrapped the cross he brought with him in a piece of cloth and left it in front of his father's quarters at the foot of the door, then left the house without saying a word to anyone. As he reached the summit, he stayed far back

enough from the edge to prevent the chance of falling
down again for the third time. Sitting waist deep in a daisy
forest of white petals, he marvelled at the numbers of
the small single yellow eyes, facing upwards and sending
homage to the sun. From his vantage point he couldn't see
the sandstone cliff so he just sat there soaking up the beauty
of nature, amazed at all the colours looking back at him.

Blue tits perched above hopped from branch to branch
with great minute agility, tweeted like crazy, informing
the rest of the bird and animal kingdom the stranger was
back in town. A lone buttercup stood out amongst the
daisy world, on top worked and buzzed a busy honey bee.
Attached to its hairy legs hung little yellow bags of pollen,
collected by endless hours of hard work, resulting in the
wrapped finished article fit for its queen. The boy wanted
a closer look at the honey sacks, and as he clasped the bee
into his hands, the ground under him gave way, hurling him
forward and downwards…again.

Grasping at fresh air with his arms outstretched, he
managed to release the bee into the air as he bounced,
bumped and catapulted all the way to the bottom. As
he came to a sudden stop, mother duck and her dandy
darling ducklings darted forward in disbelief. He offered an
apology but she turned away and left with her tail in the
air. Since he was there, he decided to climb up and enter

his den once more and after his usual finger grappling climb, he squeezed through the crack in the sandstone and vanished from the outside green world.

Once inside, he sat with his knees pressed against his chest and covered his eyes with an arm, all of his built up emotions then exploded from his stomach. Travelling faster than an arrow to the back of his throat and escaping through his mouth, he sobbed because he couldn't understand what he was sobbing for and his eyes welled up and overflowed, causing them to drip continuously until he cried his heart out…then cried a little more. In his heart he was in a place jammed between a rock and a hard place, when he should have been celebrating, instead he was in mourning.

Placed within a tomb in a rich man's dream, he was the loneliest boy in his gold paradise, all these riches to buy the world and he struggled hard to find it within himself to create even the smallest of smiles. Gaining favour in fathers eyes was important for wee Bruce. He always felt good when his father seemed proud or pleased with him, and having his name being used in vain upset him. It was all supposed to end in celebration and pride, he hoped to be held shoulder high in achievement and congratulated by all, his name being spoken around all of Scotland.

Instead, all went sour, a very anti-climax clouded his

expectations and he'd never felt lower in spirit than he did at this moment. Growing up was hard, and this wouldn't be the first or last time he'd feel like this.

Through his frustration he kicked out at a huge bulging sack, spilling out coins in various directions, causing one of the smaller gold pieces to dance in a spin. Observing the money dance for a moment diverted the boy's attention away from his hurt, until the coin fell flat and then fell silent.

Suddenly a voice from outside called his name. It was close by and he recognised it…it was his father. He quickly shuffled to the entrance and peeked his head outside. His father was not yet in sight but he was close around the bend. Pulling his head back in he decided to remain silent. As his father edged closer to the boy he leaned forward enough to watch him with one eye, probing him closely as he slowly walked past, checking the ground for signs as he went. From his side hung a freshly filled canteen of cold water, causing wee Bruce's tongue to run along his dry bottom lip He was really thirsty. From his parched mouth came the words.

"Father, father I'm up here. Come and get me."

His father stopped in his tracks, re-traced his steps and stopped at the sandstone. He still couldn't make out where his son was. Scrutinising the area he looked confused as to where the sound was coming from.

"I'm up here father."

"Robert!" his father shouted, "Where are you son?"

The boy popped his head out waving his arm.

"You alright?" asked his father.

"Don't know," answered the boy, his bottom lip trembling.

"C'mon down son," he said, pulling the cross out from under his top, "I guess you found this up there with the other things?"

"Doesn't make any difference does it?" he pleaded, "You said you wished I'd never found the coin. Everyone's arguing over it and half the village are going crazy because of it." He wiped a tear with his knuckle, "I don't know what I found, the world's gone mad and it's my fault…it's a curse."

His father sat at the streams edge, being careful not to lose his focus upon his son. "I'm sorry you had to hear that from my lips, it wasn't aimed at you, this has nothing to do with you and there is no blame."

His father stood up and walked over to wee Bruce, looking up he threw the cross up into the boy's hands.

"I don't give a damn about this. This is not what I'm about and I don't need it in my life."

The boy caught his crying eyes in the reflection of the cross.

"How did you get up there?" his father queried.

"It wasn't easy," replied the boy.

His father wasn't as agile as his son but he finally reached the opening in the rock. His body wouldn't squeeze through the crack so he just popped his head inside, his eyes opening wide as the treasure was displayed out in front of him.

"Right, get yourself down," he insisted.

"You're not getting any of the gold?" asked wee Bruce.

His father gave him his hand to help him out, "I've seen enough already, let's go."

Down below he put his arm around the boy's shoulder and leaned his head against his sons. They both sat at the waters edge looking up at the wall. As wee Bruce sipped at his water, his father laughed.

"I'd never have found that in a million years, how did you know?"

Wee Bruce pointed to the sky.

"They helped me."

"You're a remarkable boy," said his father, I'm so proud of you as my son.

"What you heard me saying earlier wasn't aimed at you in any way, you must understand that…I was showing my displeasure at other peoples' reactions to greed.

"The world can keep their treasures, my treasure in life is my family and that gold up there couldn't pay enough for them."

His father placed the coin into his small hand and closed his fingers around it.

"What do we do now?" asked the boy.

His father shrugged his shoulders. "It's your choice. You found it."

Wee Bruce stood up and with a single attempt, threw the coin up and into the crack in the wall. His father nodded, "I was hoping you'd do that." The boy then sprinted along the edge of the stream shouting… "Last one back to the house is a hogs head."

His father finally caught up with him, grabbing him and placing him under his arm, and as they made their way home the bluebottles returned to their feast in the den and the ducks enjoyed their peace.

The coin and other treasures were never spoken of again and to this day remain where they were found.

THE END

Paul Victor Hunter

Paul was born in Robroyston, Glasgow in 1962 shortly before his twin sister Donna.

He studied Media and Communication at Clydebank College in Scotland and is an award winning short film maker through his writing and as an actor. Paul also studies Scottish history and culture, and participates in living history events. Inspired by the 19th century fairytales and folklore created in Germany by the Brothers Grimm, Paul has branched into writing childrens' fictional short stories and poetry.

As a younger man, Paul spent several years as a fashion model, before moving to Belgium. There, he lived the bohemian life style as an artist for seven years with exhibitions in Antwerp and Brussels. He speaks Flemish and Dutch.

At an early age Paul obtained the gift of spiritualism and has used these psychic experiences to write his 'Wee Bruce' short stories. They focus on a 'gifted' boy who accepts his fate during the medieval period, and through hardships is helped and influenced through the spirit world.

OTHER TITLES FROM AUCH BOOKS.....
From Greek author Konstantina Ritsou

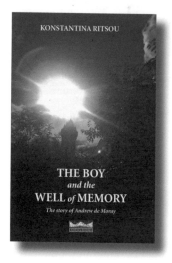

'The Boy and the Well of Memory' is by Greek author Konstantina Ritsou. For the first time it tells the story of Andrew de Moray, joint Guardian of Scotland with William Wallace and co-commander of the victorious Battle of Stirling Bridge. RRP £11.99. Visit our website to find out more, where you can also buy the book.

'Looking for William', also by Greek author Konstantina Ritsou, is a theatrical composition from Shakespeare's texts. It is an engaging take on the life and times of William Shakespeare. RRP £9.99. Visit our website to find out more, where you can also buy the book.

www.auchbooks.co.uk